MARGARET WILD & KERRY ARGENT

RUBY ROARS

For everyone who likes to roar – MW

Margaret Wild and Kerry Argent are donating a portion of their royalties to the Tasmanian Devil
Facial Tumour Disease Project through the 'Save the Tasmanian Devil Appeal' (University of
Tasmania Foundation, www.tassiedevil.com.au)

This paperback edition published in 2009

First published in 2007

Allen & Unwin
83 Alexander St
Crows Nest NSW 2065
Australia
Phone: (61 2) 8425 0100
Fax: (61 2) 9906 2218
Email: info@allenandunwin.com
Web: www.allenandunwin.com

National Library of Australia
Cataloguing-in-Publication entry:

Wild, Margaret, 1948-
Ruby roars / Margaret Wild ; illustrator, Kerry Argent.
ISBN: 978 1 74175 752 1 (pbk.)
For children.
Argent, Kerry, 1960-
A823.3

Cover and text design by Kerry Argent and Lisa White
Set in Minion at 20pt over 30pt.
Printed in China at Everbest Printing Co

10 9 8 7 6 5 4 3 2 1

Illustration technique: Kerry Argent used watercolours and coloured pencils to illustrate this book.

When she was a baby, Ruby liked making popping noises with her dummy.

'Pop! Pop! Pop!'

And gurgling noises. 'Gurgle, durgle, furgle!'

And giggling noises.

'Hee hee hee ha hee!'

But now that she was older, Ruby liked making scary noises.

'**Scrrr!**' she said.

'**Screekle!**' she said.

'**Scrunch!**' she said.

'That's the idea,' said her mum.
'Good try,' said her dad.

But neither of them
looked at all alarmed.

'Shivers!' said Ruby,

and off she went to practise being scary.

'SCRRR!' Ruby shouted.

'**SCRRR** to you too,' said Owl, with a silly swoop.

'ScrEEKLE!' Ruby shouted.

'ScrEEKLE bleekle fleekle,' said Fox with a grin.

'S̲CRUNCH!' Ruby shouted.

'SCRUNCHY wunchy,' said Bull, with his mouth full.

'Shivers!' said Ruby.

    She couldn't scare anyone, not a frog, not a fish.

Ruby listened. There were noises all around her:

crick, CRACK,
squawk, squeak,
snuffle,
snort.

What noises could *she* make?
wondered Ruby.

And she opened her mouth wide to find out…

Ready to rip and roar,
    Ruby hurried home.
        She tiptoed into the kitchen…

'SSSSSCCREEEOOOOW! SCREEEOW!'

she howled.

'Oh, Ruby,' said her mum, 'I've spilt
the knucklebone soup – you gave me such a fright!'

'Good,' said Ruby.

Taking a deep breath, she tiptoed into the lounge-room…

'YEE-OOWW-EEE! YEE-OWW-EEE!' she howled.

'You little devil!' said her dad. 'I've dropped
   three stitches – you nearly scared me out of my wits!'

'Excellent,' said Ruby.

'My turn,' said her mum.
'My turn,' said her dad.

'SCRRUNKLEGROOO!

SCRUNKLEGROOO!'

they both howled.

And they chased Ruby round and round the cave,

until they caught her,

and hugged her,

and put her to bed.

Just before she went to sleep,
Ruby stuck her head out of the window.

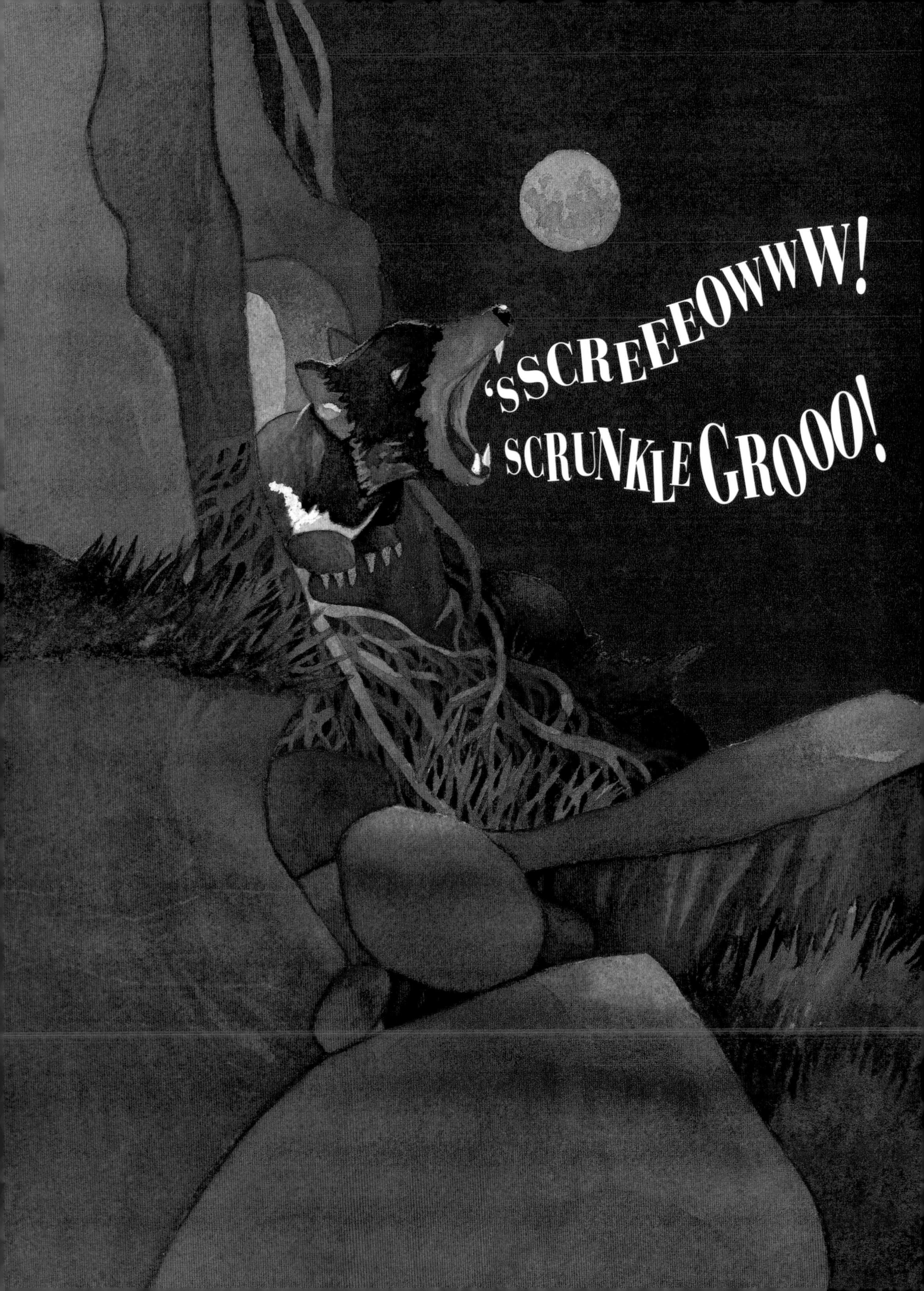
'SSCREEEEOWWW!
SCRUNKLE GROOO!

YEEE-OWW-EEE!
YAMMER-AMMER-OOO!'

she roared

into the night.

And far away, Owl, Fox and Bull trembled.
'Who was that?' they asked, because
they knew it couldn't possibly be little Ruby…

…could it?